# I AM Just a Dot

by **Shatton A. Claybrooks**
Illustrated by Autumn Draper

AuthorHouse™
1663 Liberty Drive
Bloomington, IN 47403
www.authorhouse.com
Phone: 833-262-8899

Because of the dynamic nature of the Internet, any web addresses or links contained in this book may have changed since publication and may no longer be valid. The views expressed in this work are solely those of the author and do not necessarily reflect the views of the publisher, and the publisher hereby disclaims any responsibility for them.

Any people depicted in stock imagery provided by Getty Images are models, and such images are being used for illustrative purposes only.
Certain stock imagery © Getty Images.

This book is printed on acid-free paper.

ISBN: 978-1-6655-5375-9 (sc)
ISBN: 978-1-6655-5376-6 (e)

Library of Congress Control Number: 2022903991

Print information available on the last page.

Published by AuthorHouse  03/10/2022

authorHOUSE®

# Dedication

This book is dedicated to the Most High Yah, Creator and Maker of all things. It was inspired by His Set-Apart Spirit (Holy Spirit).

**Isaiah 48:13** "My hand (Yod) surely founded the earth, and My right hand (Arm/Yahusha) has stretched out the heavens; I called to them, they stood up together."

# Special Thank You

I would like to send a special thank you to my awesome and amazing illustrator and sister in the faith, Autumn Draper!!!

Thank you for bringing my vision to life, as according to the leading of the Set-Apart Spirit of Yah and His word.

# Prologue

The main character of this story, Period, will have body limbs that represent the pictographs of the original (paleo) Hebrew letters Yod, Bet, and Hey.

**Hebrew Letters and Meanings:**

**Yod**- The Hebrew letter "yod" is a pictograph of an arm and hand.The meaning of this letter is to work, make, do, help, power, authority, and throw, as when one praises. These words indicate the power, authority, and functions of the hand. It is also spelled "yad," meaning hand. It is the 10th letter of the Hebrew alphabet.

**Bet**- The Hebrew letter "bet" is a pictograph of a tent. The meaning of this letter means house, tent, family, with, in, and inside. The family resides in or inside of the house, and is therefore protected and safe. It is the 2nd letter of the Hebrew alphabet.

**Hey**- The Hebrew letter "hey" is a pictograph of a man with his arms raised up.The meaning of this letter means to behold, look, breath, sigh, reveal, and revelation from the idea of looking at a great sight by pointing it out. It is the 5th letter of the Hebrew alphabet.

## Main Character's Body Limbs

**Yod**- (يـلـ) - Periods arm/hand
**Bet**- (لِ) - Period's shoes
**Hey** (ﻉ) - Period's feet; When Period's shoes are off, look at the revealing of his feet.

# Vocabulary Discussion

**Unique**
**To be separate; rare; exclusive;**
**different; privileged; CHOSEN**

Teachers/Parents, please engage your students in explicit, systematic vocabulary instruction for the highlighted word **BEFORE** reading this story. Provide examples, show pictures, or have them do think alouds or turn-and talks to help them understand what it means to be unique. Allow them to identify what is unique about each character or even themselves; students can even compare and contrast to elevate their understanding. Finally, have them identify words, phrases, or sentences within the text that show a character being unique.

"I am just a dot," said Period.

1

"I am not like the question mark, and I am not like the exclamation mark. I don't do anything exciting. I am just a plain old dot," said Period.

"I can't get humans' questions answered, and they can't count on me when they are excited or need to express strong feelings."

2

3

"Who would want to use me when they write? I am useless," said Period, as he held his head down towards the ground.

Period walked away in great sadness. He always knew that he was different, but he did not like being different. He wanted to be like the other ending punctuation marks.

"There is nothing special about me. There is no strength in my size. Why am I so small and boring? " Period thought.

Period often imagined himself solving problems and having the **unique** shape like the question mark or the enthusiasm of the exclamation mark. He never saw his own uniqueness, though.

However, that was not going to stop Period. He was determined to be different. Period dressed himself differently.

He took baths at different times.

For breakfast, he even ate his cereal in different ways. "Milk, today, and orange juice, tomorrow!" Period thought loudly to himself, but nothing worked. Period was still a dot.

9

Period was very sad. So, he decided to take a walk to the park to make himself feel better. The park was Period's favorite place to go when he needed to think or relax.

Upon arriving at the park, Period spotted two of his writing classmates, Question Mark and Exclamation Mark. They shared the same last name for a reason.

They were brothers, and they were also the most popular ending punctuation marks in the land of writing. Every human loved using them when they had something important to write.

Period joined Question and Exclamation by the goodly tree.

"Hi, Period. What's wrong? Why are you looking so sad? Did something happen? Are you ok? Do you need help?" Question asked really fast.

Exclamation sighed, "Oh, my goodness!!! Do you have to ask so many questions?"

"Do you have to always overreact?" Question sarcastically clapped back, as he pointed at his brother.

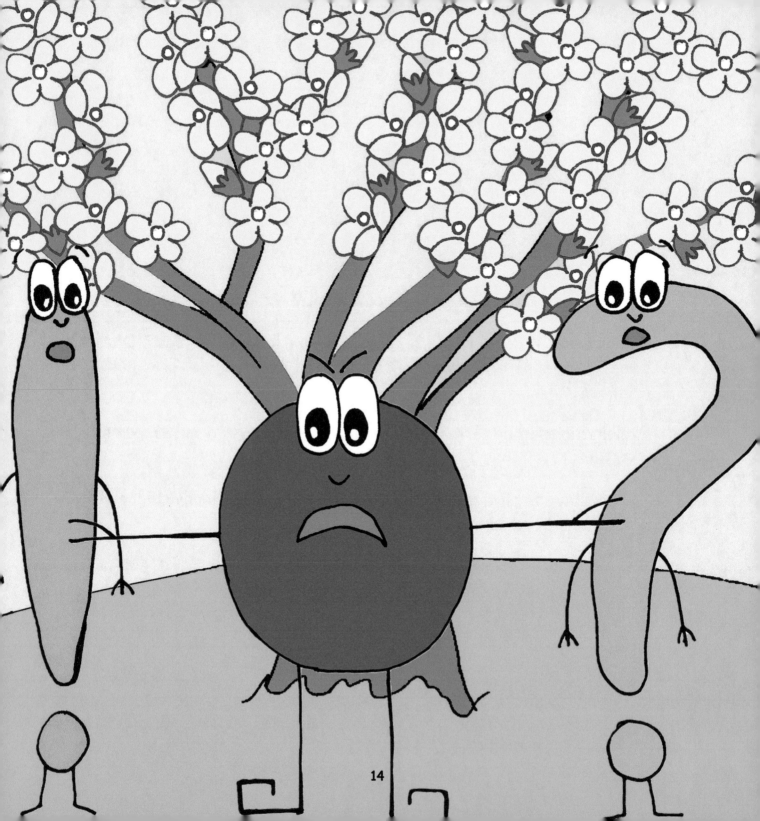

14

Period had heard enough of Question and Exclamation bickering with one another. They had quickly forgotten that their friend was in trouble.

"Hey, guys! Seriously? I'm the one with the problem, remember?" Period intervened, annoyed at this point.

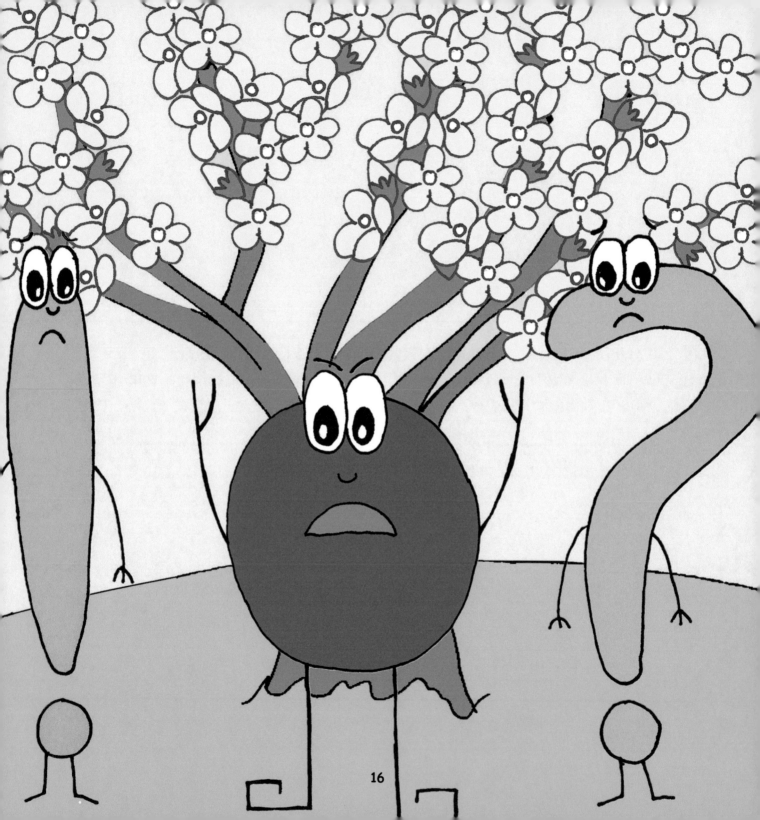

16

"You guys have no reason to be attacking one another. All the humans love you. You both have **unique** shapes and add so much more than I ever could to the land of writing."

"Like I said before, and I'll say it, again. I am just a plain old dot. I don't do anything special," said Period.

18

Question turned to Period and said, "Now, wait a minute, Period. Don't be so hard on yourself, buddy. You are more valuable to humans than you think."

"Yeah! Without you, humans wouldn't know when to stop when they were completing a thought or a sentence," Exclamation added, trying to cheer Period up.

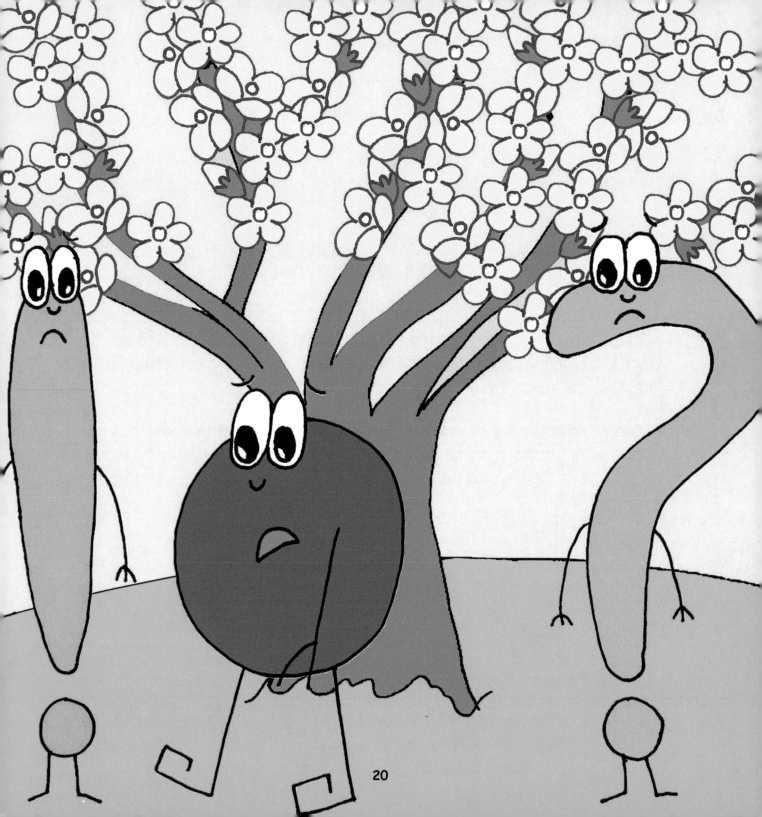

20

Unfortunately, nothing worked. Period refused to listen to them. Question and Exclamation had failed to cheer up their good friend. Now, everyone was sad.

"I am just a plain old dot," Period repeated, feeling hopeless and walking away.

"No human will ever need me. I'm useless and bring no value to writing!" Period loudly sighed.

Just when Period began to walk away, he heard a loud yelling sound.

"Help!!!" Period heard as the sound got closer. It was his favorite human, Judah.

"Oh, no! That's our friend, Judah. He's in trouble!" Period said with an elevated voice.

Judah needed help. A bully had just stolen his blue bike.

"What's wrong, Judah?" Question asked, trying to get an answer out of him. "A bully just stole my blue bike!" he replied, crying.

"Oh, no!" yelled Exclamation. "It's a good thing the Punctuation Department is located on the park. Let's go!" said Exclamation, showing strong feelings.

Period, Question, and Exclamation walked little Judah over to the Punctuation Department.

"Our friend has just had his blue bike stolen. Can you help him?" Question questioned.

"Yes! We need answers, now!" said Exclamation, expressing himself strongly.

"Hey, little Judah! I'm Sergeant Exclamation, and I give all the orders around here. Detective Question will look for clues to find your bike, but Officer Dot will need a statement from you, first," said Sergeant Exclamation.

Officer Dot gave Judah a pad and a pen and told him to write a statement. Now, Judah was not that good at writing. He needed his friends to help him.

Thank goodness Question and Exclamation were there to help, but Period remained quiet while they tried to help Judah. They tried and they tried, and they tried again, but Question and Exclamation could not help little Judah write a statement.

"I can't help little Judah write this statement!" Question said, frustrated. "That's not what I do! Officer Dot isn't asking him questions. Judah has to tell what happened; he has to explain how his bike was stolen," Question continued.

"Yeah! I'm so angry right now because I want to help, too, but I can't! Officer Dot is looking for a statement of the events that took place. He needs exact details, not our personal feeling on the matter," said Exclamation.

"I am just a question mark," said Question. "And I am just an exclamation mark!" Exclamation emotionally expressed out loud. "We really need you, Period! Only you can help little Judah get his blue bike back where it belongs!" they begged.

34

Period was almost on his way out of the Punctuation Department when he finally realized his worth.

"You're right, Question and Exclamation! I am the only one who can help. Making statements is what I do! I not only let the reader know when a sentence is finished, but I also give the reader important information that they need," shouted Period.

36

"Little Judah needs me! I have to save him! I won't let him down," he promised.

Period helped little Judah write a very detailed statement about the events that took place at the park. He helped him give important details that assisted Detective Question in cracking the case.

Three days later, Officer Dot caught the bully and returned little Judah's blue bike back to him, safe and sound.

"Yay!!! Period saved the day!" they yelled.

Period, Question, and Exclamation were all so happy that they could help Judah out in his time of need, but they refused to take any credit. They gave all praise and honor to THE DOT. For, surely, his hands did all the work.

At last, Period finally realized his worth in the land of writing. He hadn't considered how coveting had robbed him of appreciating his own gifts.

"Although small, I am the most commonly used punctuation mark in writing. I am not boring after all! For, I DECLARE ALL THINGS! **I DECLARE THE WRITTEN WORD!**" Period shouted, standing on a rock.

"**I AM** a **DOT**, and **I AM POWERFUL!**" Period believed with all his might.

The End

**READucation Consulting**
Visit the website:
www.reaaducationconsulting.com

READucation Consulting is an intensive reading clinic, providing a literacy-based focus on reading education and development. Our top priority is to develop and support high levels of proficiency in reading awareness. In general, clinicians collect data, employ evidence-based practices, and measure outcomes to assist them in making informed decisions, such as the diagnosis and treatment of their patients. Consequently, this is the reason why we utilize the clinical approach. We use valid and reliable measures that are not only research-based, but aligned with the science of reading. We believe that all students can read, and we're dedicated to helping you teach them. We help provide you with the aptitude-needed to identify, treat, and eliminate reading difficulties.

Despite countless efforts from school districts, administrators, and even state and federal legislation, scores in reading continue to drop, with only 37 percent of students reading at a proficient level by the end of third grade. This is not only disheartening, but unacceptable. Clearly, the gap between our instructional approaches and "how" our students are learning to read have widened. This is why READucation Consulting has taken a different trajectory to diagnosing and treating reading difficulties. We not only utilize proven best practices, strategies, and learning techniques, but we also apply a brain-based approach, which is inclusive of the science behind "how" students learn and process information; hence, tapping into the best way that students learn to read. We are committed to transforming the literacy experience for those who are cultivating the minds of our future.

# About the Author

Shatton A. Claybrooks is the author of the heartfelt, Detroit-based novel, "Second Time Around." By profession, Shatton A. Claybrooks is a District Literacy Specialist & Coach for a Michigan charter school district. She is also the Founder/CEO of READucation Consulting, an intensive reading clinic, providing a literacy-based focus on reading education and development. She founded READucation Consulting for two reasons. First, she is beyond passionate about EVERYTHING literacy! Second, she wanted to share the expertise and training that she mastered in the beginning of her teaching career with novice and experienced educators who are struggling to teach reading. Visit the website: www.readucationconsulting.com

As an educator of 26 years, Shatton holds an Associates Degree in Liberal Arts, a Bachelors Degree in Social Science, specializing in Sociology, a Masters of Arts Degree in Education, specializing in

Curriculum & Instruction, as well as a Masters Degree in Education, specializing in Elementary Education.

Shatton is a bible teacher who enjoys reading the word, cooking new dishes, spending time with her very close friends and family, and teaching the Torah and Hebraic roots of the faith in Messiah.

Printed in the United States
by Baker & Taylor Publisher Services